Dark

By

Author of *Nightbeast*
Duane E. Coffill

This is for my family; I love you with all my heart. This is a revision of the original work from 2014. I would like to thank my father in law, Timothy J. 'Leary III for editing and revising this story.

Dark Voices

Ben Jacobs and his family moved into the Skillings' house on Wardtown Road in Freeport. It was five miles from the North Freeport General Store. The store had been there for over thirty years and also had been owned by the Skillings, but now, the Jacobs owned it.

Ben was twelve and had a younger sister, Frida, who was seven. His mother and father had bought the house for an undisclosed amount of money. The house, having been built 50 years ago, had had many owners. During those years, the home had been renovated three times.

"Ben, how come your room is bigger than mine?" Frida asked while looking at both of their rooms. "I'm the oldest, that's why. So get used to it!" Ben replied seriously. She looked at him, stuck her tongue out and turned away.

His room contained an attic with a fold-down stairway that had to be pulled by rope to gain access to it. He had three shelves made out of oak and two doors on each side of the room. The door closest to his bed led to the living room, while the other opened into Frida's room.

The carpet was tan and had been freshly shampooed by the real estate company that was selling the house for the Skillings. The plaster on the ceiling was touched up with a hint of 'fresh paint.' The room also had two closets, both walk-ins. *This* isn't bad, *as long as I have room for my PS4 and Xbox One game systems,* he thought to himself.

As the day went on, Spring filled the crisp air. It was

March with a few months of school remaining. Even though he had moved, Ben hated his school, which was now, located four miles away.

He was going to school the following day, but still had a lot of unpacking to do. There were eight boxes sealed with tape and containing video games, his clothing, and his two very important video game systems. **Game**s and **Systems** contents were identified on the sides with a black marker. Ben sat down and used a jackknife to open the boxes. The knife had been given to him by his Grandfather

Grandfather Leon was his mother's father. He was eighty when his heart gave out and was found dead laying on his side on his bed three days later with his eyes and mouth open, and his right-hand clutched to his heart.

Leon was close to Ben as they used to go walking in

the woods and find different shells from shotguns used to hunt deer and rabbits. When he had passed two years ago, Ben was crushed and kept to himself for a while. He cried a lot but never expressed his feelings of loss to his parents.

The boxes with his game systems were heavy.   As he was cutting the edges to complete this tedious task, he sensed someone watching him. Both of his room doors were closed. Ben stopped abruptly and looked around, but didn't see or hear anyone. He sat with his jackknife in his left-hand.   The box he was cutting was half opened.

Ben continued to look around. He glanced upward at the closed attic door and sat there gazing up at it.

Ben got up and slowly knelt by his half-made bed. He slowly looked under the box spring to see if anything or anyone was there. Nothing, he turned to look at the closet. The door was slightly open. He walked towards the door while holding the jackknife tightly in his grip. Ben felt his heart pounding faster and faster. He opened it quickly and . . . Nothing!

Ben closed the door after checking behind some clothes hanging from their plastic master. He closed the door, sat down near the boxes and continued opening them. After two straight hours, he was almost done. He had hooked up his game system and played for a while without his parents' knowledge.

He fell asleep on his bed while he was waiting for dinner to be ready. The smell of American Chop-Suey permeated the air while Ben was asleep. He dreamed that his video games were becoming *dust collectors* and that his mother was throwing them out.

Ben slept for two hours. He woke up when he felt his foot being tugged on. His mother stood at the foot of his

6.

bed and said, "Dinner is ready, Ben." She smiled as she looked around his room and was visibly pleased with Ben's unpacking effort.

Rubbing his tired eyes, Ben got off the bed and almost tripped over the empty boxes. He walked into the living room and saw his father and his sister at the kitchen table, already indulging themselves in the delicious meal.

"Is your room all set, Ben?" His father asked while filling his plate. Ben nodded. His father smiled a little but knew he had been playing his video games *As long as the work was done and Ben's room was reasonably tidy, there was not going to be an issue,* His father thought.

Ben grabbed a can of soda from the fridge and sat down with his plate in front of him. The padding on his seat showed engraved roosters. His mother loved roosters. There were paddings, paintings, and Tupperware of roosters everywhere! His father would just roll his eyes and go with it.

Ben scooped up his food with garlic bread and melted butter...*Damn! My mother cooks an awesome meal!* He thought. "Thanks, Mom for making this."

She looked at him and said, "You're welcome Honey! I know it's one of your favorites," she said smiling while getting her plate ready.

Ben devoured his food! Between his video games, the unpacking and the nap...he was hungry!

His sister looked at Ben and gave him a *nasty look.* He looked back at Frida and knew she wasn't happy about him getting his way about dinner because she wanted meatloaf, which was her's and their father's favorite. The meatloaf would have to wait until

8.

His sister, Frida looked at him and said, "Ben's doing dishes right?" she asked her mother while eating her salad.

"He is doing dishes as well you are, Frida," their mother said while finishing her meal.

"That's not fair...this is Ben's meal and..."

"I won't have any of that, Frida!" Her mother said, cutting her off.

Frida stopped and sat in her chair. She wasn't happy because she wanted her favorite .

"We'll have your meal next week and stop giving Ben a dirty look, Frida! Her father said while drinking his soda. Frida looked at her father and said nothing, but focused on her meal.

The kids finished their meal and did the dishes as

9.

their mother instructed. Later on, their parents were out in the garage talking about things while Ben and Frida were doing the dishes while exchanging dirty looks.

They finished their chore and went to their rooms. Frida was playing with her toys and then she heard voices coming from Ben's room. She opened the door and found talking to his action figures. "GET OUT, FRIDA!" Ben yelled.

Frida giggled and closed the door. She couldn't believe he was talking to his action figures. She heard him doing sounds and voices. The walls in their new house were thin obviously. She could still hear him, although he made it a point to quiet his voice as he was not aware of how loud his voice had been.

Ben fell asleep with his action figure loosely gripped in his right hand. He woke up around 2:00 AM. when he thought he had heard something. Peering, bleary-eyed, into the inky black room, he could see that he was alone. Ben climbed out of bed and went to Frida's bedroom door. Peeking in, he saw that she was sleeping soundly, clutching her doll close to her as she slept.

Ben went back to his room and lay silently in bed. He fell asleep and dreamt good dreams while his TV cast its flickering glow around the room. The house was still and silent except for the gentle hum of the refrigerator and the groaning creaks as the house settled.

As Ben slept soundly, the attic door began to creak open. Each step began to warp and bend as something unseen descended from the attic.

Ben suddenly jack-knifed, sitting bolt upright in bed. He squinted as his eyes adjusted to the dimly lit bedroom. In his half-awakened state, Ben could have sworn that the flickering images on the screen were partially blocked by something. There was no light or light reflection off the shiny-glossy wall. He looked around and felt something near him. Ben froze with fear and suddenly felt the bed go down a little as though someone was sitting at the edge of the bed where his feet were.

"Hello..." He said quietly. "Who's there?" There was no reply. Panic began to build, and he stifled a scream. "Mom...is that you?...Dad?" his voice taking on a higher pitch as fear coursed through his body. The weight at the foot of the bed suddenly lifted. In the darkness, Ben could feel the presence of someone near him. He could sense it. His bedroom door flew open.

"MOM!" He yelled as he jumped from the bed and ran into his parent's room.

"What's going on, Ben?" His mother asked, bewildered. "I got up to use the bathroom, and I heard

12.

you," she said. She felt him shivering and took him into the living room. As they sat down on the sofa, the attic door quietly closed

"What's going on, Ben?" she asked with concern. He looked at her with fear and tearing eyes and said, "I sensed or felt that someone was in the room with me,"

"Honey, all of us were sleeping, and everything is OK."

"Mom, listen, it felt like someone was in the room with me," he said again trying to convince her.

He clutched his mother tightly. She had never seen him this scared. "Honey, let's go check it out."

He didn't want to, and with a great sense of fear, he followed her lead and walked back to the bedroom. She turned on the light and, as she suspected, there was nothing to be seen. The attic door was closed, and his bed was how he left it. She got him a glass of water while he sat on the edge of his bed and looked around. He was worried about what might happen during the night. "Mom, I could swear someone was in here with me."

She looked at him briefly then checked the closet and under his bed. She looked up and saw the attic door was locked. "Ben, there's nothing here for you to worry about. You need to go back to bed." Her voice was firm. He tried to argue, but in the end, he relented. After finishing his glass of water and laying down for a brief moment, Ben's mothers shut off the light. Ben insisted that she keep the door open a little. She looked at her Son once more before closing the door partially and went to her room.

She went back to bed with heavy eyelids and acute mental exhaustion from listening to Ben's fictional or fabricated story. She was asleep within minutes.

Ben held the covers up to his neck tightly. Like most children trying to brave the dark, his bedding was his shield protecting him from the unknown.

Ben woke up at seven the next morning and started getting ready for school. His breakfast was *Eggo's* and toast with maple syrup topping (Yummy!). His eyes were bloodshot as it had taken him a few hours to fall back to sleep. He was convinced that he had felt that something was in his room or someone...but whom?

"How did you sleep after last night's episode?" his father asked while drinking his second cup of coffee that morning and getting ready for work. Ben's father worked as a training coordinator for *ASUS*. He would go to various stores and check on sales, train local store associates and *ASUS* reps on current and new products. His job paid him

$35,000 per year, and it came with good benefits. Ben's mother, worked full time also. She was a Sales Manager at Best Buy.

"So, who or what was in your room?" His father asked with a smile on his face.

Ben's gloomy eyes looked at him and said, "It was something, but I don't know what it was..." He got up as he answered his father's question. Ben felt exhausted and all he wanted to do at the moment was going back to bed. He even thought of faking being sick and thinking...*I can pretend, and maybe Mom will let me stay home and sleep.*

"The bus will be here in fifteen minutes, so move your ass!" His mom said firmly as if on cue.

"Alright...I'm going!" he said making his way to the bathroom to brush his teeth.

Frida was ready to go. Their father brought her to school because she started at a different time., *It would be nice if Dad would do that for me.* Ben thought. Ben finished up and grabbed his school bag with his lunch included an apple, a can of *Orange Crush*, a bag of chips and two peanut butter and marshmallow sandwiches. Ben loved it when lunch time came around. His sandwiches were always squished due to his books pancaking them in his book bag. He always ended up with having marshmallow everywhere in the sandwich baggies.

He went outside his house with his lunch and thought about pretending to be sick. But then, *if I did that, they would take me to the hospital, and my parents would wonder why their son dropped in the driveway and there was nothing wrong with him. I could do it tomorrow, the same story...different day, I guess.*

His bus arrived and stopped in front of his house. He hesitated before getting on board. He climbed the dirty, metal steps and walked to the back of the bus and sat with Billy and Janice. They were both Ben's closest friends, and he had known them for four years. Billy was a year older. He liked Ben, because of his interest in video games and food. Billy's hair was charcoal black, and he had two dimples on his face and muddy brown eyes.

Janice was the same age as Ben. Her eyes were sky blue and her hair flaming red. She liked Ben...more than a friend...at least. Ben never asked, and he didn't know if she liked him that way or not.

When they sat together, it was almost always Ben and Janice while Billy got stuck sitting with some overweight or a nose-picking kid with no idea that his body and nose-picking was bad for the public eye. *And especially for the other kids that have to suffer while you demonstrate your nasty and useless talent for us!* Billy thought.

"How's the new house?" Janice looked at Ben with her innocent eyes as she smiled a little revealing her pearly whites.

"It's OK...I didn't sleep well last night." Ben said.

She looked at his dark, baggy, eyes. "How come?" she asked.

"I thought there was someone...in the room with me," he said with a little hesitation.

"You got scared? Was there anyone in the room with you?"

"Mom came in and turned on all the lights, and that was all. When it was pitch dark, it

felt like someone was on the edge of my bed...near me."

"That's creepy. Are you ok?" Her eyes locked with his.

"I'm...I'm just a little tired, that's all," Ben said.

Billy had been listening with interest to Ben's story. "Maybe it's a ghost or something." Billy chuckled.

Janice smiled, and Ben smiled a little, too. He wasn't looking forward to tonight, based on what could occur tonight. The school was long and exhausting for Ben. He wanted to go home and go to bed. His homework was light, and he could easily be finished with it within two hours.   When he got home that evening, Ben went directly to his room and started on his homework. First, it was History, then English. *Why do they give us homework? I don't know who came up with the idea, but the idea was stupid!* His TV remained off, and he put his headphones on. Doing homework was always easier with music filtering out any distractions. It also kept him from falling asleep, and he wanted to finish so that a nap would be in order. Within an hour, Ben had fallen asleep on the floor. His headphones were playing music from his iPod that had over sixty of his favorite songs on it, playing an endless jam on repeat.

His mother came in and saw that he had fallen asleep while doing his homework. She looked at him and smiled. *If he's hungry, he can warm up his dinner when he wakes up.*

While he slept with his playlist playing, it was 9:30 PM and his parents were sleeping.

Frida was still awake and reading with the TV on in the background.

Ben remained asleep with unfinished homework. When the attic door opened and the ladder went down, Ben's iPod inexplicably switched itself off. Something came down the steps, and it approached Ben. Then...something brushed against his hand. Ben woke up screaming! His room was pitch dark. He waited for his mother or father to come in, but no one did. Frida got up, and she went to his door but was unable to open it.

"WHAT DOOOO YOOU WANT?" he asked with trembling fear. Ben felt something rubbing against him, and he quickly moved, but it remained very close. He screamed again! "MOM! DAD!"

"Ben, why did you lock the door?" Frida asked loudly while struggling to open the door. "FRIDA...HELP!"

22.

Frida screamed, waking their parents. His father brushed Frida aside and tried to open the door, but it wouldn't budge. "Ben, open the door? Come on...what's wrong?" his father asked with a firm tone.

"DAD...SOMETHING IS IN HERE..." he screamed.

"BEN! OPEN THE DOOR! NOW!" He tugged at the door as his wife asked what was going on.

Suddenly, the attic door closed and his iPod came back on then, BANG! His father got through the door, almost breaking the framework. "WHAT THE HELL IS GOING ON, BEN?!" his father yelled at him as Ben broke down and cried.

His mother knelt down beside him, "Ben, what happened?" she asked softly and held him in her arms. His father was still furious but calmed down within a few minutes. He checked the door. He then realized that the door had no lock.

What the hell? Ben's not strong enough to hold this door...what the hell... Ben's father had a puzzled look on his face, and he asked Ben, "What did you use to hold the door? There are no locks on this door...what did you use?" He asked with curiosity and concern.

"That's what I'm trying to tell you...it wasn't me...it was something.." his father waved him off; he had heard enough.

Ben wanted to stay with his parents in their bedroom, but they said 'no.'

The door was left open while Frida was forced to go to bed. Ben kept his eyes wide-open and was trying to figure out, *what was going on? I can't believe my parents didn't believe me...what is going on?*

His thoughts were swimming as he searched for

answers but none surfaced.

He finally dozed off due to exhaustion and the rest of night went by quietly.

He awoke to the smell of eggs and bacon being cooked. He had two more days of school and then it was the weekend.

His eyes were heavy and droopy. His father had already eaten and taken Frida to school on his way to work. Ben was tired as evidenced by dark circles under his eyes. Going to school was something he wasn't in the mood to do.

"I'm not doing that again tonight, Ben!" his mother warned him.

"Mom, something was in my room and----"

"I don't care, Ben! Get ready for school," she said

firmly.

He nodded. He knew she wasn't going to listen to him and that telling his parents again would be a waste of time.

After taking a shower and brushing his teeth, he felt fresh as he walked out to the end of the driveway. He grabbed a blueberry muffin from his bag while outside and waited for the bus to arrive. *Would Janice and Billy believe me? Or would I get laughed at? All I know...something is wrong in my room.*

Ben waited for ten minutes. It was still a little chilly. His mother had made him wear a jean jacket with a cotton interior. He wore a black winter hat with a *WWE* logo on the front of it.

The bus pulled up with the brakes *screeching.* The exhaust coughed black smoke indicating that the bus was due for a tune-up. He waited for the door to open and the same old bus driver smiled at him as he got on. He sat with Janice who smiled at him. Billy was almost sleep in the hard-leathered and cold seat.

"Did you sleep well," she asked kindly while looking at Ben with sparkling eyes.

"Janice, I didn't sleep well, and the night didn't go well at all!" His reaction was to hide the truth, and he didn't even know how to tell Janice the truth if he *could.*

"What do you mean? Did you finish your homework?" She was fishing for answers, Ben knew. He wanted to tell her but would she believe him?

"What do you mean, Ben?" she asked again, knowing Ben was hiding something.

"You can't laugh or make fun of me," he said with a serious tone."

"Ben...it's me! Remember?"

"Alright---I think there's a ghost or something in my room," he said with a little hesitation. He still wasn't sure if it was a good idea to tell her. She looked at him, smiling. "Really?" she asked softly.

He looked at her and saw that she was serious. "I think, whatever it is...it comes out at night. It has been next to me these past two nights and then, last night, the door was locked, and my parents couldn't get in. Afterwards, we saw that the door had no lock or anything." He was scared and shaking a little after just thinking about it.

"Ben---we need to do somethin' and do it fast!" she said with concern.

He looked down with a very serious expression but felt better after telling her.

"We need to know what is going on with your room. Have you checked online about that house?" she asked.

"No, I haven't had the chance. I just don't know what to do. My parents don't believe me, and Frida just likes it when I get into trouble." Janice put her hand on his, and he felt the comfort and softness of her hand. It assured Ben that everything would be alright.

"Maybe, we can come over and see if anything happens," she suggested while watching other kids getting on the bus. The school bus continued to make a horrible *screeching* sound every time the bus driver would use the brakes. Billy opened his tired eyes and asked, "What's going on?"

"Did you hear what we were talking about?" Ben asked firmly.

Billy looked and said, "Yes."

Janice said to Billy, "We need to go to Ben's and see what's up with his room, are you in." She asked while her hand lay gently on Ben's.

Ben smiled. He didn't move his hand away or feel *icky* about Janice putting her hand on his. He liked it because he felt comfortable and he knew she would do whatever it took to help him. He looked at Billy who was all set for going over to Ben's. But Ben's parents had a strict curfew for his friends visiting, especially on school nights.

"Billy, we're going over tonight! I can sneak out and you can too, right, Billy!?" Her eyes locked with his and wanted an answer.

Billy looked down at the gray, track-like, streams that helped school kids keep their feet grip on the floor from slipping when it's wet. "I think I can get out; I'll let you know by tonight, Janice." His voice filled with concern and fake courage as he was worried about getting caught.   Janice didn't care; she wanted to know what was going on in Ben's room and she wanted to help.

After ten minutes of hard questioning and the threat of Janice's foot going up Billy's ass if he didn't want to help, he agreed to go with great reluctance.

Janice turned and looked at Ben, "We'll be over later tonight after our parents fall asleep."

"Thanks, Janice...I appreciate it!" She smiled as she kept her hand on Ben's. He just sat next to her feeling content.

"I'll be by around 8:30, Billy. It will take us about a half hour to get to Ben's and then that will be it. The window in your room will be perfect for us to crawl through and see what is going on. I'll also do some research on your house, too!"

"Thanks, Janice! Please don't wait until midnight or anything; it will be too late" he said while smiling. He was afraid, though, of what could happen or, *if* anything would happen. He just didn't want his friends to think he was crazy or something. His concern was that nothing might happen at all.

"Thanks, Janice...and you too, Billy! he said with relief in his voice.

"No prob!" Billy responded.

"Anything, Ben." her hand left his as they were getting up and walking off the bus. He looked at her and smiled. Her eyes locked with his and smiled kindly. Billy followed her while taking out a note with his locker combination code on it because he still couldn't remember the code after all these months.

"Everything will be fine after tonight," she smiled

sweetly. Ben felt a little relieved but was still worried. The two left while Billy finally won his *tugging the lock on the locker war* and then left to go to his classes.

During the day, Ben thought about what could happen that night. He was afraid of putting his friends in danger. Also, how would they handle their parents? *I can't believe they're coming over tonight. If they get in trouble, we're screwed!*

He went to his last class of the day and got on the bus. The other kids were screaming and yelling. The driver grew annoyed and began yelling at them.

Ben rode home alone on the bus. Billy and Janice had been picked up by Janice's mother.

Ben got home while dealing with a slight headache. He went right into the shower. He let the hot water soothe his neck and the back of his head. He thought

33.

about tonight. *Janice said they would be here by 9:30, but what happens if they don't or can't show? Maybe she'll email or call me?*

That night, Ben ate dinner with the family. They had chicken (partially dry) because his father did the cooking while his mother was out. He went into his room and did his homework. He couldn't believe how much math he had to do.

Twenty minutes later and I'm only on question 5...I love doin' homework! His inner-sarcasm eased his frustration. He kept looking at his clock with the funny hands. It was a *smiley face* with funny fingers, and it would point towards the time...*stupid clock!* It was 9:30. *Where are they?*

He wondered when or if they would show? Just then, he heard a knock on his window that gave him a scare. He turned and saw Janice at the window sticking her tongue out at him. He smiled and walked over to the window. When he opened it, a cold breeze blew into his room.

"I didn't think you guys would show? He said while helping Janice in. Billy almost tripped, nearly giving away their intrusion "Shhh! Billy! We don't want to wake my parents," Ben said while smiling and rolling his eyes. He was glad to see his friends.

After warming up a little, Billy looked around. Janice looked at Ben with a look of concern on her face. Ben could see the concern.

"I did some research on this house from the internet, and I will tell you, Ben...it's interesting...." Her words dug into Ben's skin like a tick embeds itself. "Back in 1962, a man named, Carl Waterstone was the owner of this house, and he had a little girl, her name was Stacy. When she was ten..." Suddenly, the lights went out in the room, and they all screamed!

"Holy shit! What the hell just happened!?"
Billy said, trembling.

Janice stood close to Ben; she could feel him shaking.

Suddenly *"Beeeennnnnyyyyyy..."* A voice said from
the darkness.

"What do you want?" Janice asked bravely, with a
firm voice.

Ben said nothing. Meanwhile, Billy was almost
making fresh lemonade in his pants.

"Billllllyyyyy..." The soft voice said. Billy and Ben
trembled with fear and Janice put her arms around them.
They all held each other while this was going on.

"Janice see....you brave girl...I see you...." The voice
said while a cold wave of air washed over them. They

held each other tighter. Janice wanted to tell Ben about what she had found out, but that would have to wait.

"I KNOW WHAT YOU WANT! YOU CAN'T HAVE IT!" Janice said firmly and loudly.

"What do you mean? What does it want?" Ben asked while holding Billy who was shaking so badly. "I will tell you in a second," she said.

"HOLY SHIT! IT'S GOT ME! HELP ME!" Billy yelled. There were sounds of a struggle. Ben and Janice felt Billy being *pulled* from their grip. They lost him in the inky black that enveloped them. Billy continued to scream for help. Shadows shrouded him, but his screams remained as beacons of terror in the darkness.

"BILLY....WHERE ARE YOU?" Ben yelled. They tried reaching out to him in the dark, but his screams were moving around, as though he was being dragged around the room. It was almost as though something was playing games with them.

"LET HIM GO! LET HIM GO!" Janice yelled.

Suddenly, a loud *THUMP* was heard, and then the lights came back on. Billy was lying face down on Ben's bed. There were scratches on his back, more like claw marks.

His face was turned away from Ben and Janice.

"Billy?...Billy?...Are you OK?" Janice asked softly, Ben and Janice held each other tightly. She walked closer to Billy, who was not moving. Janice got closer. She reached out and touched his back. He was cold. She reached up and grabbed him by the shoulder.

"OOOOOOOOH NNNOOOOOOOOOOO!" Billy screamed. The sound he made was monstrous causing

Janice to scream. She jumped back against Ben, knocking him down.

The two of them sat on the floor with Ben holding Janice in his arms.

Billy slowly got up with his face remaining hidden from them. They began to scurry backward as Billy stood silently in place facing the wall.

Suddenly, the door burst open with a bang and Ben's parents rushed into the room.

"What is going on here?" Ben's mother demanded.

"You two...I'll take you home!" his father said, angrily. As Ben's father spoke, Billy dropped like a bag of potatoes.

Billy got up shaking a little but was OK.

"Let's go!" Ben's father said once more. Janice looked at Ben while Billy was scratching his head and didn't know what had happened."

See you at school, Ben," Janice said.

Ben nodded, and his father took his friends home. Ben was grounded for two weeks, which meant no video games and no internet. That night, Ben's father arrived home from dropping the *young ghost investigators* off at their homes. He went into Ben's room. Ben was cleaning the mess that had been made. He said nothing, but his eyes locked with Ben's, *I will never find out what's going on here,* Ben thought. *No internet and no video games...Might as well just bang my head against the wall and do homework for the rest of my life!* Ben's father left Ben's room after he saw Ben was cleaning the mess and he said nothing to Ben about tonight.

The next day, his sister just smirked knowing her

brother got in trouble by having friends over without their parents' permission. Ben said nothing and remained focused on his cereal. He soon left to wait for the bus. The bus *roared* up to his driveway, and he got in. Neither Janice nor Billy was there. *Maybe their parents were informed about last night over at my house? I wonder what happened to Billy and Janice? I hope my Dad didn't say anything to their parents, because if so, they'll never be able to come over again. I would only see them at school.* The bus arrived at the school and Ben walked into the building with the other kids screaming and throwing paper balls in the hallways. Still, no sign of his friends.

He went into his homeroom and was notified by another student that his friends weren't at school today. Ben was worried. *Did I get my friends into trouble? I hope not! They didn't deserve that. It's my fault!* He was thinking about what Janice had been telling him before the "*ghostly*" interruption. She had been talking a little about the history of the house, *did she know the history of the house? If so, what was it?*

That night he fell asleep in bed watching TV. His homework for that night had been completed. His head rested peacefully on his white-fluffy-pillow. He dreamt that his friends were in his window, and, as they were climbing in, something from the darkness pushed them off and they landed on a pallet covered with spikes and nails, and it was revolving like a wheel.

They hit with a *crash!* Their bodies were torn to pieces like paper being fed into a shredder. Ben could hear their screams as the dark figure turned to look at Ben before slowly walking towards him. Ben could only see the cloaked figure as the face was hidden, but the smell of rotting flesh filled the air.

It lunged for him! He jumped! He woke up,

sweating! He didn't scream, but he was covered with sweat. He wiped the sweat from his face with an old shirt that was on the edge of his bed.

His eyes stung from the perspiration. He got up off the bed and felt the cool air on his sweat-soaked back. He went to the bathroom, pushed his shorts down little, and he relieved himself. The stinging feeling was intense as his bladder was full. He finished, and he wiped the rim and the bottom part of the toilet with toilet paper.

He finished and washed his hands and went back to his room. He got into his bed and felt something watching him. He looked around while the TV was still on and playing a B-movie. Then he looked up. His mouth fell open. He saw a face staring at him, and he couldn't breathe.

The face was peering down at him malevolently from

the attic above. Ben was suddenly paralyzed with fear. He began to tremble. The warm sweat on his body turned into a blanket of cold, wrapping around his young body. "Wha....wha....do...you want?" He asked while shivering with fear.

The face was emotionless and said nothing. The pale face was a road map of red scars, and the eyes were a dark, swampy, green.

Ben watched as the dark figure slid down the ladder from the attic like a snake. He couldn't believe what he was seeing, *Oh, my God...Mom, Dad? Where are you? Help!*

His thoughts pounded within his head. The dark figure approached the edge of his bed before disappearing. Ben stared at the foot of his bed.

"*BOO!*" It said as the face loomed out of the

darkness. It looked at Ben and smiled a little as it slithered fluidly onto the bed.

It moved toward Ben who couldn't do anything because of his intense fear. He looked at the figure's red marks and saw blood seeping through the wounds. "What are you?" he asked with a little courage, halting its advance.

"What do you want? Why are you doing this?" he asked, his voice beginning to crack. Ben watched the dark figure lick its mouth as a foul smell filled the room. Ben held his nose to cover or at least filter out the hideous smell.

The dark figure slid closer to Ben who quickly pulled his feet back from the figure. He moved back and hit the wall while the dark figure moved closer. There was barely any weight to the creature on the bed. It got closer to Ben's face with its foul stench and caused Ben to become nauseous. The dark figure's red and pale face was five inches from Ben's, and then it stopped.

It shifted its head and smiled a little revealing red-stained teeth. It glared at Ben.

"GET AWAY FROM HIM, YOU SON OF A BITCH!" Ben and the dark figure turned quickly and saw Janice holding a gold necklace aloft.

The dark figure hissed loudly and slithered quickly up into the attic. The door shut quickly with an ear-bursting slam.

"Are you OK?" Janice jumped down from the window and ran over to the wall and flicked the light switch on while Billy climbed out of the window also. She then ran over to Ben to make sure he was OK

"What happened?" he asked still stunned.

"Billy and I were out today because we pretended to be sick. He and I went on a little history trip, and we found some more stuff about this house. I found this!" It was a gold necklace with small lettered initials on the heart. The three letters read as STY. As Janice was explaining what she had found, Billy got out of the window while eating a candy bar. Ben was very happy to see them both.

"So, what does this mean?" Ben asked while getting up and scratching his head.

"This necklace, we have to give it back to Stacey. I believe she's up there" pointing to the attic.

Her father Carl was murdered by an evil man named Victor Munson. He killed Carl out of revenge because Carl had slept with his wife. One night, he came in and shot Carl four times and then, he cut off his head with an ax. Victor then killed Stacey and took her necklace."

Ben was taking in the information and asked, "How did you get the necklace?" Janice looked down at the floor and said, "My grandfather killed Victor. When he was a police officer, he felt Victor was guilty after being let go. He subsequently shot him and burned his body. When he killed him, he found the necklace in Victor's right pocket and knew he had done justice. I found the necklace in my grandfather's old toolbox in the basement after some are digging around and asking my parents. The research validated the murders."

Janice said with sadness. Ben couldn't believe it. His mouth was wide-open in disbelief. She looked at Ben and admitted, "My last name was changed, because of what he did. My mother has this wooden tool box with fish on it, and I found it. I did the research and found more information after Billy and I went to the Freeport Cemetery on Wardtown Road and put two and two together."

Her words were filled with fear and disbelief. She also told him that other people had lived at the house and three different reports of hauntings had been reported. The children of those families were reported missing and had not been seen since.

"Shit! We have a lot of work to do! We have to return this necklace to Stacey or Carl?" Ben looked at her and asked, "How?"

She looked at him while sitting on the bed and pointed to the attic. The two boys raised their eyebrows and Billy was shaking his head. *So, what the hell was that in my face?" Ben asked.*

"That was Victor. He was protecting his property." Her words rolled off her tongue like aircraft launching from an aircraft carrier. "We're heading up now," she said while gathering a crucifix from her jacket.

Ben looked at her and nodded. Billy didn't want to go, but what choice did he have? The three of them gathered their things and pulled down the ladder after ensuring that every light was on in Ben's bedroom. The ladder pulled down heavily. Ben led the way.

He felt his heart was about to burst out of his chest like in the A*lien* movie. He climbed the ladder with Janice following close behind. Billy was shaking badly, afraid of being attacked again.

"How are you doing, Billy?" Ben asked while reaching the attic.

"I'm almost shitting my pants...but otherwise, doing fine." Janice and Ben smiled.

"We're on top, now what?" Ben asked while helping Janice into the attic with Billy following with great hesitation. A light bulb was hanging a few feet from them, and Ben went to reach for it. Something slowly touched his arm, "HOLY SHIT...SOMETHING TOUCHED MY ARM!" he said loudly.

"Shhh, Ben! We gotta be quiet, or we'll wake your parents!" Janice said as she touched his arm. The contact was reassuring to Ben. She reached for the light and turned it on.

They looked around. Ben had never got the chance to check out the attic. Billy spotted something in the corner of the attic and yelled, "WHAT THE HELL IS THAT?!"

Janice put her hand over his mouth. She took out the necklace from her pocket and kept it in front of her as she anticipated Victor jumping out at her.

Billy remained behind (by the ladder), as Ben followed Janice. As they moved forward, they saw what

Bill spotted in the corner. Something pacing slowly back and forth. They edged closer. The light was swinging gently showing a man who had been hanged. His body swung back and forth creating a grotesque scene.

Janice winced while Ben held her as she kept the necklace in front of her...then, suddenly, the body stopped swinging and dropped to the attic flooring while landing on its feet with its back to them. The man turned around. It was Victor. His face was blushing evil! "It's him...holy cow!" Ben yelled.

Victor stood staring at them, his eyes filled with blood as he grinned at them. Drops of blood drooled from his mouth. His hands were pale, and his nails were made of blood and mold. The dead-flesh smell grew thicker and thicker.

"WHY ARE YOU DOING THIS?" Billy screamed.

He rushed down the stairs and, in so doing, fell and hit his head on the bottom rung knocking him unconscious.

Janice now understood. It was Victor who Ben had encountered in his room. This was no man...he was pure evil! "BILLY?!" Ben yelled for his fallen friend but received no response.

Victor stood still and enjoyed the fear displayed before him.

"WHAT THE FUCK ARE YOU?" Janice yelled. A gentle and cold hand touched Janice's arm, and she jumped! It was Stacey. Her pale, frail body stood still while looking up at Janice. The girl still had that *innocence* about her.

"Are you Stacey?" Janice asked while Victor was slowly moving towards them.

"He killed my Daddy and I...he did it!" she said while

pointing at Victor. "Daddy and I have seen Ben...I think he's cute." Her smile and voice were soft. Ben smiled while Victor moved swiftly toward Ben and pushed him to the attic floor. Victor, with an evil grin, stared at Janice. He ignored Stacey who screamed for him to stop! "DON'T HURT THEM!" She yelled.

Victor ignored her as Janice kept backing away. She was reciting verses and holding the gold necklace in front of her. Victor stopped.

"Daddy, where are you?" Stacey said, crying, knowing her new friends were in trouble.

"GET AWAY FROM HER...YOU FUCK!" Ben lunged at Victor.

Victor caught him with his right-hand and held him by the throat. Janice threw the necklace at Victor who grinned devilishly. Stacey couldn't do anything. She called for her father to come and help. Ben, meanwhile, was choking as Janice continued to yell at Victor to let Ben go. Suddenly, a hand grabbed Victor by the throat, and he dropped Ben.

It was Carl! Stacey's father. "You are no longer the owner, Victor. It's time to go," he said. Carl picked up Victor by the throat and brought him back to the rope that he hanged Victor with. Carl wrapped the rope around Victor's neck.

Victor screamed, and blood gushed out of his mouth. Carl then pushed Victor through one of the windows with the rope wrapped around Victor's neck. The glass shattered.

Ben got up. Carl stood staring at the window that showed blood on its jagged edges.

Carl turned to Stacey and said, "It's time to go." He

was ready to move on Janice looked at Carl and thanked him. Carl turned his eyes toward Ben and Janice and nodded. He smiled a little when he reached out for Stacey, who had picked up her necklace from the attic floor. She took her father's hand, and they walked to the shattered window. Stacey turned to look at Ben and winked and then, Stacey and Carl vanished.

Ben got up while feeling disoriented. He went over to Janice, gently grabbed her hand, looked at her, and kissed her.

"Thank you," Ben said.

She looked at him and said "Why are you thanking me...I didn't do much."

"I would have never gone up here and who knows what would have had happened later," Ben replied.

"I hope Billy is OK," she said with concern while

smiling at Ben. They held hands and walked over to the ladder.

Billy was rubbing his head and looked up at them, "No more! I'm either going home or to the damn hospital!"

Ben and Janice chuckled a little. Ben helped her down.

That night, Ben went to bed and fell asleep...but with one eye open...

Author's Note.

This story was originally written back in 1992 during my senior year in high school. It was called, "Voices In The Room" and when I re-wrote it, I decided to change the name. Thank you for buying and reading my story, and I hope you enjoyed reading it as much as I enjoyed writing it.

Duane E. Coffill

8/28/2017

Other books and stories by Duane E. Coffill

1) "Cursed Darkness."

2) "The Eyes Within."

3) "Nightbeast."

4) "Infamous Fear."

5) "The Path" is currently being edited.

6) "Rest Area" will be edited next year.

7) "Northern Frights" anthology by the Horror Writers Of Maine. Check out "Window Of Darkness" by Duane E. Coffill in this awesome anthology.

Websites/Social Media

1) Twitter.com/DuaneECoffill

2) www.facebook.com/horrorwriterduaneecoffill

3) duaneecoffill.weebly.com

Biography

He was born in Brunswick, Maine on September 4th, 1973. He grew up in Freeport, Maine. He grew up reading horror, suspense, and his favorite novel is "Salem's lot" by Stephen King. He also loves movies! He loves all kinds of horror, action, suspense, and even, romance movies with Shelley. He graduated from Freeport High School in 1992. He began writing at the age of twelve and has written and published three novels and four poems. His fifth book, "The Eyes Within" is available in paperback and Kindle versions. He is an advance in computers and computer software with over fifteen years experience in various computer training programs. He is the Founder/President of Horror Writers Of Maine, Horror Authors Alliance and is a proud member of New England Horror Writers. He has recently self-published his first book, "Cursed Darkness" for the Kindle and print versions. His second revised novel, "Nightbeast" is available now. His organization, Horror Writers Of Maine just published their first anthology called, "Northern Frights" which was published by Grinning Skull Press. He is at work on two novels and three short stories. He currently resides in Windham, Maine with his beautiful wife, Shelley. He also has two beautiful daughters, Madelyn and Savannah and he sees them weekly.

Made in the USA
Columbia, SC
06 August 2021